JPicture Tusa.T

Tusa, Tricia.

Bunnies in my head /

c1998]

DATE DUE	
DEC 2 6 2002	OCT 1 0 2004
APR 0 4 2003	
	JAN 2 0 2005
APR 2 7 2003	MAY 1 7 2005
MAY 3 1 2003	AUG 2 - 2005
MAY 3 1 2003	NOV 2 3 2005
JUN 1 1 2003	
SEP 1 1 2003	MAR 9 - 2006
JUL 3 7 2004	
JUL 3 - 2004	
	MAR 2 0 2007
JUL 0 3 2007	MAY 2 2 2007
	AUG 1 3 2007

DEMCO, INC. 38-2931

JUL 0 5 2011

Brittney

J.P.

Munirah

JEANINE

Marion

AARON

Sarah

Kelly

Richard

Benny

Gilberto

Julian

JESSE

Mercedes

Jeremy

Beth

Alexandre

Tiffanie

Alexandre

Carrie

Kalani

Melissa

Bunnies in my Head

By Tricia Tusa

with art from

Children of M. D. Anderson Cancer Center

BUNNIES IN MY HEAD is a long-dreamed-of project celebrating the artwork of
pediatric patients at M. D. Anderson Cancer Center. Its publication is a collaboration
of many volunteers and staff members at the Children's Art Project, working together
to create a dream:

- author and illustrator Tricia Tusa
- editor Lucy Herring Chambers/The Bedford Book Works, Inc.
- graphic designers Chris Hill, Linda Hofheinz
- advisors Roni Atnipp, Malinda Crain, Roseann Rogers
- the art volunteers who have given their talents and time to the children
  through the years

Proceeds from the sale of this book will fund programs that benefit the educational,
emotional and recreational needs of patients at M. D. Anderson.

Library of Congress Cataloging-in-Publication Data
M. D. Anderson Cancer Center Children's Art Project/Tusa, Tricia
Bunnies in my Head: a celebration of children's imaginations/story and illustrations by
Tricia Tusa/artwork by pediatric cancer patients from The University of Texas
M. D. Anderson Cancer Center.
   p. cm.
   Preassigned LCCN: 98-87473
   ISBN #0-9664551-8-5
   SUMMARY: A young girl—representing children of all ages—explores her world,
   both real and imagined, with her paints and crayons.
   1. Art–Juvenile Fiction.   2. Imagination–Juvenile Fiction.
   I. M. D. Anderson Cancer Center Children's Art Project/Tusa, Tricia II. Title

First edition, 40,000 copies, 1998.

Printed and bound in the United States of America by Wetmore & Company, Houston, Texas.
Published by The University of Texas M. D. Anderson Cancer Center, Houston, Texas.

Requests for permission to reproduce any part of this book should be directed to
The Children's Art Project, P. O. Box 301435, Houston, Texas 77230-1435.
To order this book, call 1-800-231-1580.
www.mdanderson.org

MD ANDERSON
CANCER CENTER
CHILDREN'S
ART PROJECT

To the children of M. D. Anderson who soar
above adversity with courage and
their creative imaginations.

Their valor is inspiration to us all.

I've got bunnies in my head.
White and silent,
as big as mountains,
in search of carrots
as big as trees.

I like to paint trees.
Cold ones out in the snow
and fancy ones at Christmas time.
Trees that tower over me
like the buildings downtown.

With my brush and crayons,
I can show you another world
different from this one we live in.
A world far away
and inside my head.

One where orange, furry things roam wearing socks.

This is my cat Millie.
She is as dark as midnight.
Millie pounces on her own tail
as if she has captured a prize.
She bats at butterflies in the garden.
A fuzzy one turned out to be a moth
and changed my sweater into Swiss cheese.

This is our garden.
I think all the flowers from my favorite
nightgown faded off back here.
All the colors and light and shapes
bump into one another
and wake us up early.

This is my house
with a fence in front
and a squirrel up above.

What if I lived in a tall, skinny house
that swayed back and forth on purple stilts with a rainbow overhead?
There would be a circus underneath with a trapeze
and a dancing polar bear and carnival rides
you could roll on far into the night.

I can tell you anything with my paintbrush.
When my head feels as jumbled as that
or as still as this,

or even at bedtime when my
mom turns out the light and I feel scared,
I remember my crayons.
I think when I hold them, I sprout wings in my sleep
and am free to fly around the world and stars.

I wonder what will show up next.

A bunny!
A round, pink one with happy green eyes.
I can tell you all about him

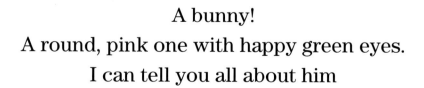

tomorrow.

AFTERWORD FROM FORMER FIRST LADY BARBARA BUSH

Tomorrow—a word filled with promise! When our daughter, Robin, was diagnosed with leukemia in 1953, there were few tomorrows for children with cancer. The extraordinary advances of medical science now offer many tomorrows for young cancer patients. The art in this book represents the work of children who have been treated at M. D. Anderson Cancer Center in Houston, Texas. It is often exuberant, sometimes thoughtful, always a reflection of their world. Collectively, it is a remarkable statement about the resilience of children, their courage and their ability to live each day. Imagine what Cody was thinking the day he found the bunnies in his head that have become the inspiration for this story! With Tricia Tusa's endearing character and insightful story, *Bunnies in my Head* is a book to be shared over and over with children, grandchildren and friends of all ages. It will encourage everyone to celebrate the joys of today and to imagine even happier tomorrows.

Barbara Bush

CHILDREN'S ART PROJECT

Since its beginnings in 1974, the Children's Art Project has been an important part of the lives of pediatric cancer patients at M. D. Anderson Cancer Center. The brainstorm of a volunteer, the Project began by printing holiday greeting cards created from young patients' artwork, netting $588 the first year for patient-focused programs at M. D. Anderson. Aided by teachers from the Glassell School of Art at The Museum of Fine Arts, Houston, the Project began to grow. Today, with the continued support of thousands of volunteers, the Project funds a wide variety of programs at M. D. Anderson every year—having raised more than $10 million since 1974.

For both volunteers and staff, the children have always been the focus of the Project. Working together, we provide programs that bridge their experiences in cancer treatment with the world of healthy children: summer camps for patients and their siblings, ski trips for amputee patients, a Child Life Program that eases the trauma for patients and their families, an in-hospital education program to help patients keep up with their peers, college scholarships and so much more.

Through the years, the Children's Art Project has celebrated with children and their families who triumphed over cancer—and mourned for those who did not. Always we are amazed at the special way each child copes with life, yet manages to laugh and to live.

THE ARTISTS OF M.D. ANDERSON

 Cody
age 10

 Brittney
age 7

 Monte
age 17

 Beth
age 11

 Brittney
age 10

 Richard
age 11

 Antonio
age 10

 Jesse
age 11

 Rachel
age 12

 Rachel
age 13

 Patrick
age 5

 Jeanine
age 18

 Melissa B.
age 10

 Lacy
age 7

 Kalani
age 11

 Melissa G.
age 15

 Katherine
age 7

 Kelly
age 16

 Kalani
age 11

 Sasha
age 5

 Aaron
age 8

 Shane
age 17

 Alejandro
age 10

 Hunter
age 5

 Jeanette
age 13

 Carrie
age 12

 Cody
age 9

 Sasha
age 5

 Hunter
age 7

 Sayna
age 14

 Brittney
age 6

 Alexandra
age 7

 Joseba
age 11

 Karissa
age 8

 Tiffanie
age 7

Allison
ELENA
Dwayne
HEATHER
Cody
Joseba
Melissa G
Monte
Alejandro
Tori
Karissa
HULTOr
Jeanette
JANEL
Sasha
ANA PAULA
Andrea
SAYNA
Lacy
Duhan
Lamautha
Katherine
Antonio
Tamika
Shane
alsh
Diana

Brittney

J.P.

Muniran

Marion

JEANINE

AARON

Sarah

Avet

Kelly

Richard

Sarah

Bonney

Gilberto

Julian

JESSE

Mercedes

WACK

Jeremy

POK

Beth

Alexandre

Tiffane

Page

Carrie

Kalani

Melissa